HANS CHRISTIAN ANDERSEN'S

FAIRY TALES

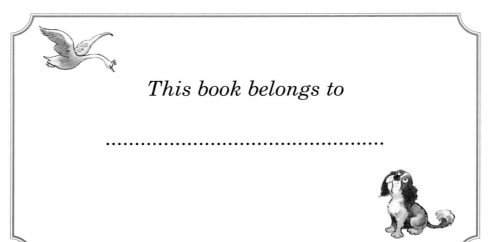

This book belongs to

....

HANS CHRISTIAN ANDERSEN'S
FAIRY TALES

Illustrated and retold
by Val Biro

AWARD PUBLICATIONS LIMITED

First published 2005

Published by Award Publications Limited,
The Old Riding School, The Welbeck Estate,
Worksop, Nottinghamshire, S80 3LR

www.awardpublications.co.uk

5 7 9 10 8 6 4
10 12 14 16 18 20 19 17 15 13 11 09

Printed in Malaysia

CONTENTS

The Wild Swans

In a country by the sea there once lived a King.

He had eleven sons and a daughter, the beautiful Eliza.

He also had a new wife, who was a wicked woman. She hated the children from the start.

She told such evil lies about
the eleven sons that, at last,
the King banished them from
his kingdom.

The Queen put a spell on the sons. They turned into great wild swans and flew out of the palace and away over the sea.

The wicked Queen told the King lies about Eliza, too.

So Eliza was sent away to live in a poor cottage with a peasant and his wife.

11

Years later, the King wanted to see Eliza.
When she came, the Queen was so filled with
hatred that she commanded three toads to
make Eliza ugly, stupid and evil.
She put the toads into Eliza's bath.

But when Eliza came to have her bath, the toads had no power over her goodness and they turned into roses.

So the Queen tangled Eliza's hair and put dirt on her face.

Then she sent her to see the King.

He did not know his own daughter and he ordered her to leave the palace and never to come back.

Poor Eliza wandered into a forest.

There, a kind old woman told her that she had seen eleven wild swans on a lake.

"They must be my brothers!" cried Eliza, and she ran to find them.

She saw the swans, with crowns upon their heads. And suddenly, as darkness fell, the swans became her own dear brothers!

The Queen's spell had turned them into swans by day, but at night they turned back into princes.

Eliza hugged them all with joy.

Next morning, they became swans again.
They placed Eliza in a sheet and flew with
her across the sea.

They landed in a far country, and Eliza went
into a cave to rest.

She prayed that she might find a way to free
her brothers from the spell.

When she had fallen
asleep, a fairy came and
spoke to her.

"Pick some nettles and
make eleven shirts with
them. Throw them over the
swans and the spell will be
broken. But, remember this,
you must not speak one
word until then, or your
brothers will die!"

Next morning, Eliza began her work. She went out to gather the nettles and soon her hands and arms were covered with blisters.

Then she began to make the shirts. She did not mind the pain because it was to save her brothers.

That night they asked what she was doing,
but she remained silent.

The youngest brother wept to see this.
His tears fell on her hands and the blisters
vanished.

Next day a hunting horn sounded and the
King of that country rode up with his men.

He was enchanted by the lovely Eliza and
wanted her for his bride.

So he took her on his horse
and rode back to the palace.
Eliza remained silent all the while.

Everyone at the palace thought
she was beautiful, except for one
wicked Minister.

"She's a witch," he said.

Eliza wept because now she could not
finish making the shirts.

The King felt sorry for her and thought that perhaps she missed her work.

So he ordered that her shirts and nettles be brought from the cave to the palace.

Eliza smiled for the first time and loved the King for his goodness.

Every night she worked hard to finish the shirts.

When there were only three left to make, she ran out of nettles.

So, in secret, she went to gather more.

She went to an old churchyard where it was said only witches lived.

The wicked Minister saw her.
"She is a witch," he told the King.
"She must go to the stake and burn!"
The King was very sad, but had to agree.
So Eliza was flung into prison, but she did
not speak one word.

In prison, she worked day and night, and ten shirts were ready when she was taken in a cart to the stake.

Even then she still worked. She had just finished the last shirt, when eleven swans came flying towards her.

As she was led to the stake, she threw the shirts over the swans. One by one, eleven handsome princes stood there.

The spell had been broken at last! And the wooden stake blossomed with red roses.

Eliza could now speak, and told her story.

The King was overjoyed and clasped her to his heart.

People cheered, birds flew in the air above and all the church bells rang out.

Dan the Dunce

Once upon a time there was a Princess. She was bored. So she decided to get married.

"But my husband must be clever and amusing," she said. "I will test each suitor as he comes."

So the news was given out by the Herald to the whole country.

Only the cleverest and most amusing people need apply.

Far out in the country there lived an old Count. He had two sons who were the cleverest men for miles around.

The count also had a third son. Nobody thought he was clever and they called him Dan the Dunce.

The two clever sons decided to become suitors for the Princess, and began to prepare for the test.

The first clever son read lots of books in Latin, and learned them backwards too. He also read all the local newspapers for the past three years.

The second clever son read lots of books on Law, and learned some jokes as well.

They dressed up in their finest clothes.
They even oiled their mouths to make them
speak more smoothly.

The Old Count gave them
splendid horses to ride and gifts
to take with them.

Everybody came to watch
them go.

"I want to go too!" cried Dan the Dunce.
"All of a sudden I feel like getting married.
I want to marry the Princess."

"Nonsense!" said the Count.
"You aren't clever enough. I won't
give you a horse or gifts to take."

"Never mind," laughed Dan. "I
shall go by billy-goat!"
And off he trotted, singing a song.

Soon he met his clever brothers on the road.

"Here I am!" he called. "And look what I have found for the Princess!"

He showed them a dead crow, an old clog and a pocketful of mud.

TO THE PALACE

"You are not clever or amusing," sneered the clever sons, and rode on ahead. They arrived at the palace gates an hour before Dan got there.

The Princess saw her many suitors in the palace hall.

In the corner by a hot stove were three Important People. They wrote down every word the suitors said.

But the Princess was bored by all of them. "No good!" she said every time. "Out!"

Now it was the turn of the first clever son.
But he was so frightened that he forgot
every word of Latin, even backwards.
All he could say was,
"It is hot in here."

"No good!" said the Princess. "Out!"

The second clever son was just as
frightened. He forgot all about the Law, and
all his jokes.

"It is *very* hot in here," was all
he said.

And the three Important People
wrote down every word.

"No good!" said the Princess. "Out!"

Then Dan the Dunce rode
in on his billy-goat.
The Princess smiled.

"I like that nice hot stove," said Dan. "I'll roast a royal chicken in it, just for you!"

And he pulled out the dead crow.

The Princess laughed.
"But we have no cooking pots!"
"Here is just the thing," said Dan,
and he showed her the old clog.
"And here is a little gravy," he said,
opening his pocket full of mud.

The Princess laughed out loud.
"Do you know that every word
is being written down by these
Important People?" she said.
She wanted to see if she
could frighten Dan.

But Dan was not frightened at all.
"If they are so important, they
should have the best!" he said.
And he threw the mud right at
them.

"Well done!" cried the Princess. "You are clever and amusing. You passed the test and I shall marry you."

So Dan the Dunce married the Princess and he soon became Dan the King.
And the Princess was never bored again.

The Emperor's New Clothes

Once there was an Emperor who loved dressing up. He liked beautiful clothes more than anything else.

All day long he stood in front of his mirror to see how smart he looked.

One day two men came to the
palace. They wanted to play a trick
on the Emperor.

"We are weavers," the two men said. "We can make you the most beautiful new clothes you have ever seen. We can weave cloth that has beautiful patterns and beautiful colours. *And* it is magical! It is invisible to people who are stupid or bad at their job."

The Emperor was delighted. "Make me some fine new clothes," he said.

He gave a big sack of money to the weavers. "Start weaving at once," he ordered.

So the two men got to work. They sat at their empty loom and pretended to weave the magical cloth.

For days they went on, pretending to weave.

Soon the Emperor wanted
to see the cloth for himself. But
he was worried.

"What if I can't see it? Then
the people will say that I am
stupid or bad at my job."

So he sent his Prime Minister instead.

The Prime Minister looked hard, but of course there was nothing to see. Now *he* was worried.

"If I can't see the magical cloth, people will say that I am stupid or bad at my job," he thought.

"Oh, how lovely it is," he said, pretending to admire the cloth and went back to tell the Emperor.

"It is the most beautiful cloth that I have ever seen!" he lied boldly.

The Emperor was delighted.
But to make sure, he told his
Chief Judge to go and look as well.

The Chief Judge looked hard, but of course there was still nothing to see.

Now *he* was worried.

"Am I stupid or bad at my job? No, that cannot be!"

So he pretended to admire the cloth. He gave the weavers another big sack of money and went back to tell the Emperor.

"It is the most beautiful cloth that I have ever seen!" he lied boldly.

The Emperor was delighted.

He decided to go the next day and see the cloth for himself.

The whole Court went with him.

"Look at the colours!" said the Chief Judge.

"The pattern!" said the Prime Minister.

The Emperor looked, but of course there was nothing to see.

"Am I stupid?" he asked himself. "Am I bad at my job? No, that cannot be!"

So he said that the cloth was the most beautiful cloth he had ever seen.

And the whole Court agreed, even though they could not see a thing.

When the cloth was finished, the two men
pretended to make the clothes.

They cut the air with their big scissors, and they sewed with big needles and invisible thread.

Soon the two men said, "Your clothes are ready."

The Emperor took off his old clothes and the two men pretended to dress him up in his new clothes.

"They are so light that you won't even feel them," they told the Emperor.

And they were right. Certainly he could not feel them. And nobody could see them either.

But everyone said how smart the Emperor looked.

Now the Emperor was ready to walk through the streets and show off his new clothes.

Everyone cheered as he passed by, even though they could not see a stitch. No one wanted to look stupid or bad at his job.

75

But suddenly a small child looked at the Emperor and cried, "He's got nothing on at all!"

Everyone heard.

They looked at the Emperor. Then they looked at each other and looked at the Emperor again.

At last all the people shouted, "He's got nothing on at all!" And the Emperor knew that they were right.

The Emperor blushed.

But he drew himself up and held his head
higher than before, and walked bravely on,
pink from head to toe.

The Flying Trunk

Once there was a banker who was so rich that he could have paved the streets with silver.

When he died, he left a fortune to his son.

But the son lived merrily and spent the money fast.

He made kites from banknotes, and played ducks and drakes on the lake with his gold coins.

Soon he had nothing left except a few
pennies and the clothes he wore, a dressing-
gown and slippers.

Even his friends left him, but one gave him
an old trunk and some advice.

"Pack up and be off," he said.

The banker's son had nothing left to pack,
so he put himself into the trunk instead.

Then he pressed the lock, and suddenly the trunk flew up in the air!

It flew up through the chimney and out into the sky above.

83

Up it flew, further and further away, until, at last, it was flying over Turkey.

There, it swooped down and landed in a wood.

The banker's son hid the trunk under a pile of dry leaves and walked into the nearest town.

Nobody took much notice of him because Turks wore dressing-gowns and slippers too!

Soon the banker's son saw a palace with windows high above.

"What palace is that?" he asked.

"The King's daughter lives there," he was told.

"A fortune-teller said that she will be made unhappy by a lover, so no one is allowed to visit her."

The banker's son went back to the wood,
got into the flying trunk and flew straight up
to the roof of the palace.

Through a window he saw
the beautiful princess asleep
on a sofa. Very quietly he crept in.

He woke her with a kiss and told her
that he was a Turkish wizard from
the sky. He spoke so sweetly that
she was enchanted.

Then he asked her to be
his bride, and she said, "Yes!"

"You must come on Saturday to meet the King and Queen," she said. "They love to hear stories, so tell them your best tale and they will surely let me marry you."

She gave him a sword covered in gold coins.
"I shall bring no other present than
a tale," he said, and he flew
back to the wood.

He sat on his trunk and
tried to think up a story. It was
hard work, but at last he thought
of one.

Then off he went to buy a new
dressing-gown with some of the gold.

Soon it was Saturday.

The King and Queen and the whole Court waited eagerly to hear the wonderful tale.

And indeed the banker's son told such a lovely magical story that they were all enchanted.

"Yes, yes," said the Queen. "You shall
certainly marry our daughter! We shall have
the wedding on Monday."

Next day, there was fun and dancing in the town. Cakes and buns were thrown from windows and children hopped about trying to catch them.

The banker's son bought
fireworks of every kind, and put
them in his trunk.

That evening he flew above the town and let them off.

Oh glory, what a wonderful sight it was!

The Turks were amazed. "To be sure," they said, "this is a real Turkish wizard who will marry our beautiful princess!"

The banker's son left the trunk in the wood and returned to hear what the people were saying about him.

"A wizard!" they said.

"With a beard like flowing water!"

"Wrapped in a cloak of fire!"

The banker's son laughed at how he had tricked them.

He felt happy as he went back to the wood.
But where was his flying trunk?

Alas! It was burnt to ashes. A spark from
the fireworks had set it alight.

Now he could no longer pretend to be a Turkish wizard from the sky.

He could never marry the Princess. So she is waiting for him still – and he roams the world telling tales.

The Ugly Duckling

One sunny day in summer a mother duck was sitting on her nest.

She sat for a long time and waited for her seven eggs to hatch.

At last the eggs began to crack.
"Peep-peep," said the ducklings as
they marched out one by one.
They were six of the sweetest
ducklings in the world.

But the seventh egg was big and it took longer to hatch out.

At last it cracked.

A big grey duckling tumbled out and looked around.

"Oh dear! What a large and ugly duckling," said the mother duck. "But never mind. Let's see if you can swim."

So off they went to the pond.
Splash! The ducklings jumped in
and paddled away.

The ugly duckling jumped in, too, and
swam.

"You may be ugly," said the mother, "but
you can swim very well."

The mother duck led all her
ducklings to the farm to show them
to her friends.

"What pretty ducklings," they cried,
"except that big one over there. He is a very
ugly duckling indeed!"

"He took longer to hatch," said the mother
duck. "That is why he is different."

"You are too ugly for us," said the pretty ducklings and turned away.

"You are ugly," gobbled the big turkey.

"Ugly," hissed the goose and bit him on the neck.

Nobody loved him at all.

The ugly duckling was very sad. So one day he ran far away to the marsh where the wild ducks lived.

But they turned away from the ugly duckling, too. All summer long he stayed in the marsh by himself.

In the autumn some hunters came.
Bang-bang went their guns.

The duckling ran to hide among the reeds.
But soon big, barking dogs came sniffing round
and the duckling was afraid.

"I must find a safer place," he said, and ran off to the woods.

A cottage stood among the trees and the duckling slipped in through the open door.

An old woman lived there
with a ginger cat and a hen.

"Lay some eggs for my tea,"
she said, "and then you can
stay."

For three weeks she waited
for her eggs, but of course no
eggs came.

All the while the cat
kept scratching the ugly
duckling with her claws. And
the hen kept pecking him with
her beak.

The poor duckling sat alone in a corner, feeling very unhappy.

In the end the old woman gave up waiting for her eggs, and sent the duckling out into the night.

He found a lake where he could stay to
swim around and dive.

But the leaves were turning brown, and
every day was colder.

The ugly duckling saw some lovely swans
flying high above.
"Oh how I wish I could fly away with
them!" he said.

Now it was winter and very cold. The lake was freezing over and the duckling could hardly swim.

Soon he had to stop and the ice froze around him.

A farmer found the ugly
duckling and broke the ice to
free him.

He wrapped the duckling
in his coat and took him
home for his children.

119

The children played a chasing game with
the duckling, but he knocked over a
pail of milk.

The mother screamed. "Go away! You are too big and clumsy for a pet!"

So out he ran and hid among the reeds.

121

He stayed there all through the winter.
But then the sun came out again and it was
spring.
He felt bigger and stronger.

The lovely swans came back and were swimming round the lake.

The ugly duckling recognised the beautiful birds and wanted to be with them.

So he swam out to meet them, feeling shy.
He bent his head, and in the water he saw
himself, as in a mirror.

He could not believe his eyes!
He was not an ugly duckling any more. He
was the whitest of white swans!

The other swans swam round and round
and stroked him with their beaks.
"How beautiful you are!" they said.

And so the ugly duckling, whom nobody had loved, became the happiest swan in the world.

The Little Tin Soldier

Once there was a little boy
who was given a box for
his birthday. He took the lid off
carefully and clapped his
hands.

"Tin soldiers!" he cried with
joy.

He set them out, one by one, on the table. Each one had a musket at his shoulder and they all looked very smart indeed.

The last one was just as smart, but he had only one leg. Maybe there was not quite enough tin left when he was made.

And this story is about him.

On the table there was also a pretty cardboard castle. It had a tiny lake in front of it, made from a mirror, and swans floated on the lake.

But the prettiest thing of all was a
little paper girl who stood on one leg like
a dancer.

She wore a silk dress and in her hair
was a shiny tinsel rose.

"Now, she would be just the wife for me," thought the little tin soldier with one leg.

"But I live in a box with all the other soldiers, and that is no place for her! Just the same, I would like to know her better."

So he stood behind a silver snuffbox, and gazed at the little paper dancer.

When evening came, all the other soldiers
were put back into their box and the
humans went to bed.

Now was the time for the toys to play! The
nutcrackers danced, a pencil played at drawing,
and the toy canary sang a song.

The only two who did not move were the
tin soldier and the little dancer. She stood still
on her pointed toes and he never took his eyes
off her.

At midnight – *snap*! The snuffbox opened
and a goblin popped out.

"Soldier," he said, "keep your eyes to
yourself!"

But the tin soldier pretended not to hear.

"Just wait until the morning!" growled the
goblin.

Next morning the tin soldier was put on the window-sill.

Suddenly the window flew open.

Maybe it was the wind, or maybe it was the goblin, but the tin soldier fell far into the street below!

The little boy rushed down to look for him, but it was raining and he could not see.

The tin soldier just stood there, upside down, with his musket still at his shoulder.

When the rain stopped, two boys found him.

They made a paper boat and sent the soldier sailing down the gutter.

He was afraid, but he stood in the middle of the boat, as firmly as ever.

Suddenly the water flowed into a dark drain.

The tin soldier wished that he had the little dancer by his side, but he was all alone.

"I must be brave, whatever happens to me," he thought.

A big water rat rushed out.

"Where is your passport?" he demanded.
"You must pay the toll!"

But the boat sailed on, with the tin soldier
standing firm in the middle.

The water rat chased after him.
"Stop!" he yelled. "Stop him! He
hasn't paid the toll!"
But the boat darted away on the
rushing water.

It flowed out of the drain and poured into a canal like a mighty waterfall.

The boat spun round and round.

The tin soldier thought about the dancer and stood more firmly than ever.

The boat filled with water and sank
deeper and deeper.

Then it tore apart!

As the water flowed over his head, the tin
soldier thought he would never see the pretty
little dancer again.

At that very moment, he was swallowed up by a large fish!

The fish was then caught and sold at
market. It was taken home and the cook
prepared it for dinner.

The tin soldier was lifted out of the fish and
taken up to the nursery. He still stood firm
with his musket at his shoulder.

Wonder of wonders! He was in the very
same room he had been in before.

There was the castle and the lake and... the
little dancer standing on her toe!

They looked at each other, without saying
a word.

And then a very strange thing happened.

The little boy picked up the tin soldier and threw him into the fire!

He did not say why; maybe it was the goblin who made him do it.

Almost at the same time, a door opened and the wind blew the little paper dancer straight to the tin soldier in the fire.

Together they burned into one flame – and were gone.

Next morning all that was found of the soldier was a little lump of tin, in the shape of a heart.

And all that was found of the dancer was her tinsel rose, now as black as coal.

The Nightingale

Long, long ago in China, there lived an Emperor.

He had the finest palace in the world. It had a beautiful garden and lovely woods by a lake.

People came from far and wide to see it. They even wrote books about this lovely place. And they wrote about a nightingale that lived and sang in the woods by the lake.

One day the Emperor read about this nightingale.

"A nightingale?" he cried. "I never knew about this nightingale. And yet it says here that her song is the most beautiful thing there is."

He turned to his Minister of State.
"I wish to hear this nightingale
tonight," he said. "Go and find her now."

The Minister of State did not even know what a nightingale was!

But he searched the palace high and low,
and half the Court searched with him. But they
could not find the nightingale.

Did anybody know where to find the
nightingale?

"I know!" said a little kitchen-maid. "I know the nightingale well. She lives in the woods by the lake and I shall take you there myself."

First they met a cow who mooed.
"What a lovely song," said the
Minister of State.

"No," said the kitchen-maid.
"That is not the nightingale.
That is a cow. We are still a long
way off."

Then they met a frog that croaked. "There she goes," cried the Minister of State. "A most beautiful song indeed!"

CROAK!

"No, no," said the kitchen-maid. "That is not the nightingale, but it is not far now."

It was evening now and at last they heard the nightingale herself. They were quite enchanted.

"The Emperor asks you to come and sing for him," said the Minister of State, and the nightingale agreed.

Everyone was there.
The nightingale sat upon a golden perch.
The Emperor sat upon his golden throne
and asked her to sing.

The nightingale sang so sweetly that tears
ran down the Emperor's cheeks.

"She must stay with us and sing each
night," the Emperor announced.

And so the nightingale stayed in a golden cage.

Every day the servants took her out to fly, held fast by a silken ribbon.

"You must never let her go!" the Emperor commanded.

And every night the nightingale sang.
Her lovely music filled the Emperor with
joy.

One day a parcel came for the Emperor. In it was a beautiful bird, made of gold and precious stones. In its back was a key.

It was a clockwork nightingale that could sing both day and night.

The Emperor was so delighted that he forgot about the real nightingale. She was sad and longed for her home.

So the little kitchen-maid opened up her cage and away the nightingale flew, back to the woods by the lake.

The clockwork bird had one song only. He sang it all the time, and as he sang his tail went up and down.

"This bird is even better than the first," said everyone.

And the Emperor kept winding him up and the bird kept singing.

A year went by.

Then, one day, the clockwork bird cracked and broke.

He could not sing a note.

The clock-maker mended him, but said,
"This bird is worn out. You may only wind him
up once a year."
The Emperor was sad.
"Now I have no music at all," he sighed.

Some years later the Emperor was ill. He lay in bed so ill that everybody thought he would die.

But one evening he heard a beautiful song outside his window.

It was the little nightingale! She had heard that he was ill, and had come to help the Emperor.

All night she sang the sweetest songs. And in the morning the Emperor was well again.

Ever since then the nightingale flies round the woods during the day. And every night she comes to the Emperor of China to sing her lovely songs.

Thumbelina

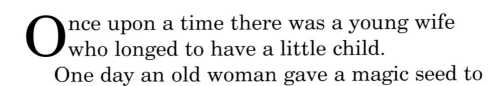

Once upon a time there was a young wife who longed to have a little child.

One day an old woman gave a magic seed to the wife.

"Plant this seed in a flowerpot and you shall see what you shall see," she said.

The young wife went home and planted it. Soon a large and beautiful flower grew out of the pot, with petals that were tightly closed. It looked like a tulip.

"What a lovely flower!" cried the wife and she kissed it.

At once the petals opened with a pop.

In the middle of the tulip flower sat a tiny
little girl!

She was beautiful, but she was no bigger
than the young wife's thumb.

So the young wife called her Thumbelina.

She put Thumbelina in a
cradle made out of a walnut shell,
and covered her with the petal of
a rose.

Here Thumbelina slept.

One night an ugly frog hopped in through the window.

"That's just the wife for my son!" she croaked, and she took Thumbelina down to the river bank.

Her son was even uglier.
When he saw Thumbelina, all
he could say was, "Croak! Croak!
Croak!"

He placed her on a lily leaf in the
middle of the river.

Thumbelina cried because she did not want to have the ugly frog for a husband.

The fishes felt sorry for her, so they nibbled through the stem of the lily and Thumbelina floated away.

She was very happy now.

As she floated along on her leaf, the birds in the bushes sang, "Tweet-tweet, what a sweet little girl!"

Suddenly a big fat beetle swooped down and carried her off into a bush.

He thought Thumbelina was lovely and placed her on a leaf.

Poor Thumbelina! She was very frightened.

The lady beetles thought that she was ugly.

"She's no good to you!" they said. "She has only two legs and no feelers!"

The fat beetle had to agree in the end, and he let Thumbelina go.

All summer Thumbelina lived alone in a wood. She ate the honey from the flowers and drank the dew on the grass.

She felt happy in the warm sunshine.

But then winter came and she nearly froze to death!

A kind old fieldmouse felt sorry for her and took Thumbelina to her warm cottage.

"You can live here all winter," she said.

Thumbelina thanked the mouse and became her maid.

A rich mole lived nearby.
He came to visit in his
velvet coat. As soon as he saw
Thumbelina, he fell in love
with her.

"He would make a fine husband," the mouse whispered to Thumbelina. "He is very rich and has a big house underground."

But Thumbelina did not want to marry a mole and live in the dark.

One day the mole took Thumbelina to his house. In the passage lay a dead swallow.

"Oh, the poor thing!" cried Thumbelina.

Later she went back alone and covered him with a blanket.

Soon the swallow shivered! He was not dead. He had just fainted in the cold.

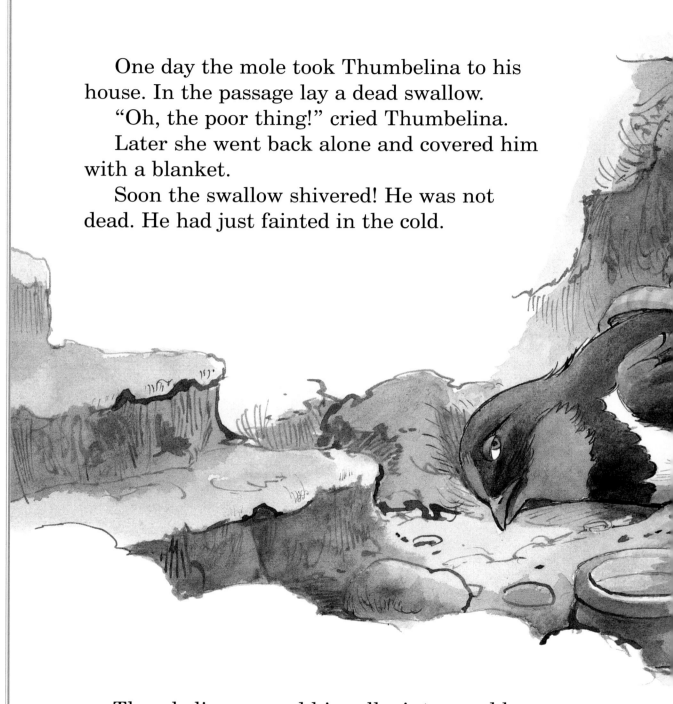

Thumbelina nursed him all winter, and by spring the swallow was well again.

"Come away with me," he said, but
Thumbelina did not want to upset the kind old
mouse.

"I cannot go," she said sadly.
So the swallow flew out into the sunshine.

All summer long Thumbelina prepared for her wedding to the mole. But she did not care for him or his dark house.

"Oh, how I wish that my dear swallow would come back to me!" she wept.

The day before the wedding, she went
out to take a last look at the sun.

"Tweet-tweet!" she heard from above.

It was her swallow!

"Come away with me, Thumbelina," he said.
"I am going over the mountains to where the
sun shines all the time."

"Yes, I will go with you!" she said with joy.

She sat on the swallow's back as he flew
high towards the countries of the sun.

Soon there were orange trees and splendid
purple grapes below.

A great white palace sparkled in the sun.

They landed near a swallow's nest.

"This is my home," said the swallow, "but you can choose a flower down there and I will put you safely on to it."

"Oh, that will be lovely," cried Thumbelina, clapping her hands with joy.

She chose a tall lily near some stones and the swallow placed her gently on its leaf.

And in the lily stood a fair young prince. He had wings on his shoulders and he was no taller than herself.

"How handsome he is," whispered Thumbelina to the swallow.

The Prince thought that she was the most beautiful girl he had ever seen.

He placed his crown on her head and asked her to be his bride and Princess of the Flowers.

He gave her wings like his own, so she could
fly from flower to flower.

"You will no longer be called Thumbelina,"
he said. "We will call you Maia, instead."

And so it was that she lived among the
flowers, happily ever after.